The Princess and the Giants

the Princess and the Giants

and the Giants

Zilpha Keatley Snyder
illustrated by Beatrice Darwin

Atheneum 1973 New York

To the memory of a kindly giant

Zilpha Keatley Snyder

The Princess and the Giants

Long ago, when magic was everyday, instead of maybe, there lived in a small kingdom, a princess, who was as beautiful as a peach orchard in April, or sunrise after rain.

The princess lived, of course, in a huge castle, bigger even than McIver's barn, with a moat around it where swans floated, and a garden with fountains, and up above reaching higher than the pines on South Mountain, a great forest of thick towers and thin spindly spires.

High up in the tallest tower, the princess had a room that was hers alone. And it was there she kept her private throne—and her royal bed, which was hung with canopies of gold and red and periwinkle blue. And on the foot and head there were carvings of all her favorite things—peacock tails and lambs and angel wings, all entwined in wild rose vines.

The princess had, of course, a thousand royal robes from which to choose, but all that fur is hot for everyday and weighs a lot, and you could lose the jewels. But always, even when she went to play, she wore her veil and crown. The veil fell down, sheer as a silver rain, fine as a thread spun from the raveled edge of a summer cloud.

There was a window ledge in the high tower where the princess, looking down, could see for miles around her kingdom reaching to the edges of the sky. Watching from on high, the princess saw a thousand things, both wonderful and strange.

She saw green garden paths where lords and ladies walked among flowers and fountains. And courtyards where knights and kings talked of great deeds done in battle, or of the beauty of their noble steeds.

But when the sun burned low through shadowed skies, the princess sometimes heard strange cries, and there appeared below things to be whispered of with fear.

For there were in the kingdom some things that were not beautiful or good. The princess knew where, in a deep wood, there was a cave full of gray wolves who waited for all who wandered by. And she had seen a strange and evil thing fly on soundless wings out of the darkest hollows of the sky.

And all too well the princess knew where, in forbidden meadows, the air was heavy with the smoke of dragon's fire.

But all these dangers dire, the princess feared not. She was so brave that nothing made her much afraid, except perhaps, the giants. For in those days the world was full of giants who ruled all the land by their great strength and size—and who daily hunted princesses, with loud and angry cries.

All things in the kingdom feared the giants, even the strongest and the very brave. The princess feared them for she knew what they planned. She knew they meant to take her to their dungeon cave where, by a cruel enchantment bound, and stripped of honor, veil and crown, a princess could be turned into a slave.

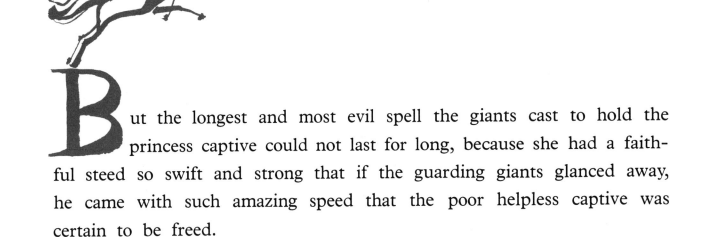

But the longest and most evil spell the giants cast to hold the princess captive could not last for long, because she had a faithful steed so swift and strong that if the guarding giants glanced away, he came with such amazing speed that the poor helpless captive was certain to be freed.

is name was Silver Arrow, and his mane was like a flame. He
was so fleet and faithful that the princess did not fear to ride
him near the greatest dangers. Sometimes she galloped by near the awful
cave of darkness where the hungry gray wolves lay, waiting in the shadows
to spring upon their prey.

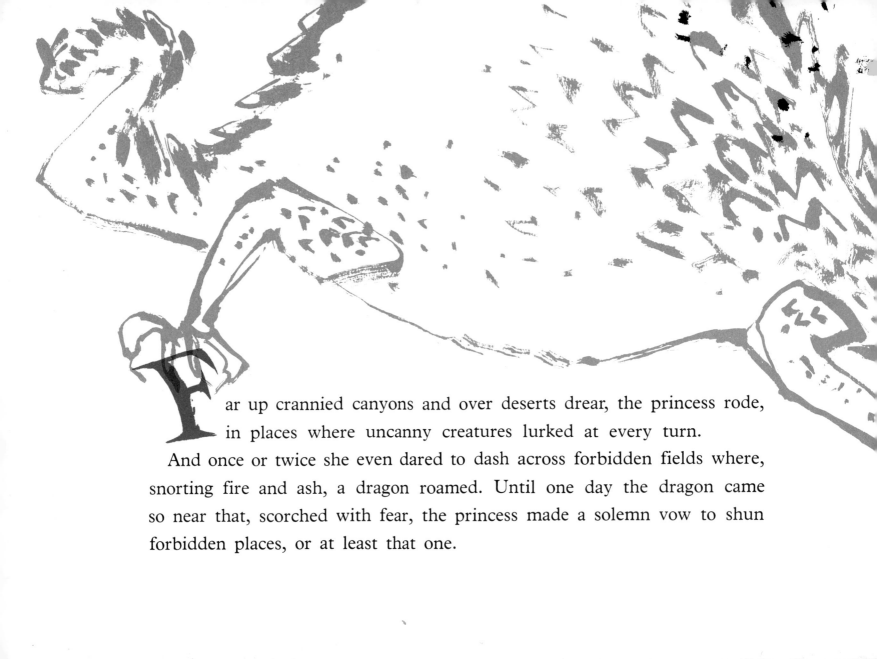

Far up crannied canyons and over deserts drear, the princess rode, in places where uncanny creatures lurked at every turn.

And once or twice she even dared to dash across forbidden fields where, snorting fire and ash, a dragon roamed. Until one day the dragon came so near that, scorched with fear, the princess made a solemn vow to shun forbidden places, or at least that one.

Weary from adventures one warm day, the princess and her charger fell asleep in a soft bed of hay, and woke to find deep shadows everywhere. From here and there through the surrounding gloom came nightmare noises, creaks and squeaks, while through the air, small winged goblins gibbered in their flight. And it was then that eyes gleamed just overhead, and a harsh voice screaming asked them WHO was there. The princess, jumping from the hay, mounted her fearless charger and sped away.

There was, quite near the castle, a high mountain, and on its peak, held captive by enchantment, there sat a silver bird.

In her dreams the princess often heard the captive speak to her and ask her aid.

"If you are not afraid," it said, "to climb the slippery mountain to the peak, your kiss upon my silver beak will set me free."

And that was why a giant, glancing toward the sky one day, saw high above the earth, the princess, just as she almost reached the silver bird.

Before nor since, a louder screech has not been heard.

o it was then that the princess knew that danger waited far below her on the ground.

A throng of giants gathered round and, watching as she slipped and slid, they shouted louder at everything she did, until the sound became a roar.

It didn't seem to matter to them that her hands were sore or that her knees were raw and red. For when the head of all the giants caught her, he just wounded her far more.

So on that dreadful day the princess, hurt and angry, made a vow to run away from her poor kingdom where cruel giants held such power. All through that night she lay awake, and at an early hour she rose and, packing all her royal clothes, she left her tower by faint morning light. Down creaky castle steps she crept, let down the drawbridge, and began her lonely flight.

The princess journeyed many miles through country that was new and strange. She trudged down level valleys and across a rolling range of hills. Although she watched for them, she found no knights in armor sent to rescue maidens in distress, much less the sheltering castle of a friendly neighbor king. But she had thought to bring provisions, and so she stopped at noon and ate some bread, made bitter by the tears of loneliness.

By the time the shadows deepened and began to creep like huge gray cats across the land, the princess turned and, vowing she would try once more to learn to live at peace with the giants, she began to run back toward her kingdom. But in the dim light of the setting sun she found that nothing looked the same, and nowhere could she find a pathway leading back the way she came.

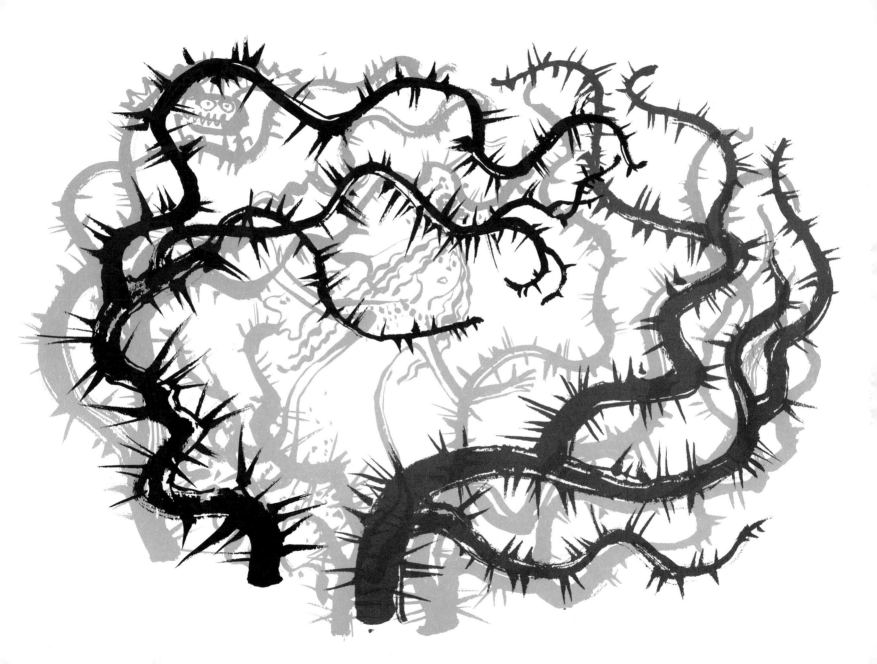

So for a long and lonely time, the princess wandered weeping, until at last, tired and sleepy, she crept beneath a sheltering ledge. For a while she slept, and when she wakened it was to strange sounds that crawled and slithered all around her in the night. She was a statue carved from fright when suddenly from someplace very near there came the thud of footsteps, and the princess wept with fear.

Something was trampling through the thicket just below her sheltering ledge. The princess heard the thick hedge shake as if it felt the weight of some enormous paw or claw or hoof. What was it? Dragon, bear or wolf? Where could she run to? Was there no way out?

But wait! Was that a light? A shout?

And then it happened, a strange and magic thing. She was rescued.

By a giant?

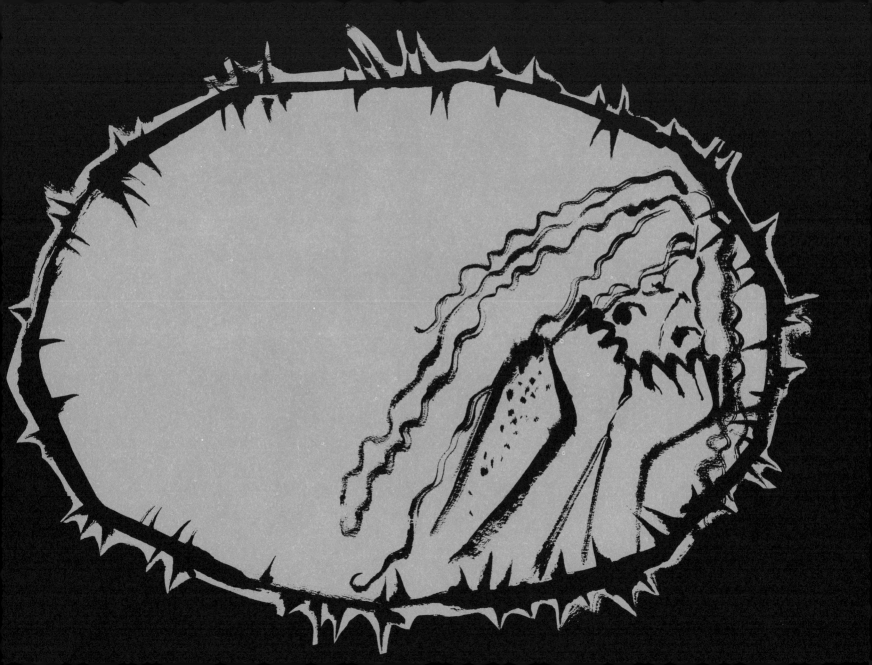

No! By his Majesty the King.